FRENCH ADVENTURES

On the banks of the Seine

Carole M. Hopkin

FRENCH ADVENTURES

Merton Press

First published 2012 by
Merton Press.
29, Brynawel,
Pontardawe,
West Glamorgan.
Wales. SA8 4JP

ISBN 978-0-9568804-0-6

© All illustrations by Carole M. Hopkin
www.morganhopkin.co.uk

To my Mother,

my inspiration.

It took me no time at all to discover that the boy I had left school for and followed to Art College was involved with a rich, blonde, and beautiful student called Miranda. With this knowledge tainting my every day and night I decided there and then to abandon art as a career and leave at the end of my Pre-Diploma year.

At my first student party I met an architecture student who knew all about films, my passion. He took me to see the latest Fellini, Antonioni, and Rene Clair, and as he had inherited a tidy sum from some relative, we dined on steak and wine while my flatmates opened another can of baked beans.

I imagined that I was in love with him, but when he left town to do his year's office practice in Germany I was determined not to remain in Britain. I would have my own foreign adventure!

Without my parents' knowledge I applied for a job as an au pair, advertised in the Sunday Times. When the letter of acceptance arrived I had to break the news to my mother that I was on my way to Paris to care for two little boys.

'But you don't know anything about children,' she said with astonishment.' What are you going to tell your father?'

I had always relied on my mother to announce any cataclysmic news to my father, and so it was that I heard his voice rise in disbelief as she told him of my decision just before tea.

When he congratulated me for my initiative there were smiles all around, and I wrote to the French family to confirm that I would arrive within the next few weeks.

In the flurry of packing I omitted to tell my parents that there were also twin girls of eighteen months to be cared for, but I thought it wiser to wait until I was actually *chez* Lestienne to let them know.

My father insisted on my flying direct from Cardiff, and although I had sworn to myself on many occasions that I would never get into a plane, there I was waving goodbye to friends and family from the steps of a late afternoon jet bound for Le Bourget airport.

I thought that my last day had come when the

2

plane began to descend minutes after we had taken off. Good heavens, it was Bristol! And then up, and down again in Bournemouth!

Awaiting my arrival was handsome Monsieur Lestienne and the two boys. *Bonjours* were exchanged with lots of smiles but the journey was otherwise silent. In the northern suburbs of Paris we stopped. Monsieur parked the car and pointed at his watch and then a nearby church. I nodded, not realising that I was going to be locked into the car for an hour while the family attended Mass.

As the time passed several attractive young men walked by and I realised how vulnerable I was on this exotic continent. The boyfriend had already faded into the ether.

I tried to concentrate on my French phrase book, realising that there was a chasm between understanding words on a page and hearing them spoken by the natives. The sky darkened and I saw the Paris of long ago.

Rue Chanoinesse
is la rue de la Colombe
A gauche, la rue Massiton
disparu.

Paris par Chs. Marville
1816-1878

THE LOST STREETS OF PARIS

2

When we finally arrive at Ablon-sur-Seine it is a relief to hear Madame's few phrases of hesitant English. She is very French, in the manner of the finest bone structure, olive-blonde skin, a Jeanne Moreau mouth and almond-shaped eyes. Unfortunately the twins are already in bed and this makes dinner embarrassingly quiet. The boys are incredibly well behaved and do not talk at table unless spoken to. Dishes are passed with lots of smiles while Madame and Monsieur exchange pleasantries and plans for the coming week. It is a simple meal of soup, quiche, salad, and fresh fruit in yogurt and honey.

Monsieur excuses himself and retreats to his study and Madame shows me my room high up in the attic. It has views over a park to the glistening Seine and in front of the window there is a desk where I know that I will read, write and draw, three passions I am determined to feed now that I am free of home restrictions and the boyfriend's critical eye.

I am hardly listening as Madame explains that

they are all awake by seven in the morning, but the message gets through that I am now under new house rules. I remember the French for alarm clock, but Madame laughs and says that she does not think one will be necessary as the children are very lively from about six-thirty. Weak at the thought of such a dawn chorus I sit down on the bed. Madame wishes me *une bonne nuit,* and leaves me to unpack.

It takes me half the night to fall asleep so that it seems like five minutes later that I hear the squeals and screams of my four charges. Surely, those cannot be the same boys who sat so angelically through dinner? I roll out of bed onto the floor and sit there for several minutes wondering if my spontaneous decision to abandon all that is familiar will turn out to be a hell or heaven?

Bea is the tomboy who adores her brother Eduard, the oldest and shyest of the boys. Pascale is the blonde angel who is always protected by Antoine, the mischievous one. Opposites attract?

I send the photograph opposite home to explain the twins to my parents. They are at their grandfather's home.

Pascale sits on his lap with Antoine next to her, while Eduard holds Bea's hand. Eduard has his mother's fine bones while the other three seem quite robust. My mother's only reaction is of shock. How will I ever manage four children? I tell her that they are no trouble at all, and explain that French homes are far more practical than British. No carpets or curtains gathering dust and germs. The floors throughout are of wood or tiles and there are wonderful shutters, which also cut down on burglaries, apparently.

Towards the end of my second week Madame suggests that I take my day off in Paris. The train takes twenty minutes and will bring me right into St. Michel. She will pack me a picnic lunch which I could have on the banks of the Seine or in the Jardins du Luxembourg.

I have been through this journey a thousand times in my mind, but as I turn on the metro steps and face Notre Dame I am completely satisfied. It is everything and more. I stand and stare as if I am willing the scene in front of me to be a reality, and it is. It is!

Wherever I turn on that amazing first day I am never disappointed. From the street market array of colourful fruit arranged with an artist's skill to the glimpses of the Eiffel Tower, I am completely nourished. A five course meal would never satisfy as much.

Walking up Boulevard St. Michel I stare at every person as if they are from another world. Well, indeed they are. They are French and they dress and talk and walk like the genuine thing.

I walk along rue St. Andre des Arts to pay homage to Picasso's studio on rue Grands Augustine, then through to Boulevard St. Germaine where I decide to have a coffee at Café de Flore.

Expensive as it is, I think of de Beauvoir and Sartre with every sip. Why wasn't I here when they were holding court, at maybe, this very table? I watch every passer-by, every mannerism, and expression from the customers who surround me.

Under a chestnut tree in the Jardin du Luxembourg I sit to have lunch - a cheese baguette, fruit and yogurt, but no wine. Ah, well, there is time enough for wine!

Very Beautiful Girls on the Boule Miche

Olive skinned
Thick Well-cut straight hair.

This Season
'de rigeur'
Long dark Cardigans
Long tartan Kilts
Flat shoes
Big bows. Hats - opt.

How I long to be SKINNY.
" " " " TANNED.
" " " " SEDUCED.
They say that the nerve endings are much nearer the surface in thin people. .: they are more Sensitive.
MAKES SENSE

©

The sun is warm for April and I spend the afternoon wandering around the great colleges of the University of Paris, the Sorbonne. This is where I would choose to study above anywhere else in the world, the heart of French academia from the C13th.

I walk through a maze of medieval streets and am suddenly out on the Quai de Tournelle opposite Notre Dame, and find Shakespeare and Co., the incredible bookshop begun by George Whitman.

Its predecessor had been at number twelve rue de l'Odeon opposite Adrienne Monnier's publishing house, *La Maison des Amis des Livres*. There, Joyce, Hemingway, Fitzgerald, Valery, Gide and many more came to talk, read, and drink.

In the bookshop I exchange a smile with an American who is asking for the best book on Parisienne life in the Twenties. Now that's my kind of man! But there is no time to linger. I have to return to Ablon.

On my next free day I take the metro to Montmartre, the mountain of the martyrs. It was so named in 272 A.D. when three saints were beheaded here while on their way to worship at the Temple of Mercury. I find the Place du Tertre where artists show their paintings on the pavement.

As I wander the back streets I see into the kitchen of a restaurant. The succulent aroma of roasted meat is too much temptation for an enormous Alsation who grabs the joint and races past me on his way to a very filling lunch. Beef will definitely be off the menu today!

Moi dans
La Place du Tertre

Mon Petit Dejeuner

CAFE AU LAIT

CONFI

14

Montmartre is inspiring, and I can't wait to get home to add some colour to my sketches. I have brought the boyfriend's present to me, a miniature watercolour set, so I thank him every time I use it.

Having exhausted my money supply I spend my next free day walking in the fields around Ablon. Amongst the corn are hundreds of poppies and I help myself to a dozen knowing that they will look glorious in the yellow vase in my bedroom. A bank rises steeply up to a high wire fence and overhead comes the roar of a jet engine gliding in to land at Orly airport. I had forgotten how close we were. Without hesitation I climb right up to the fence and sit there to wait for the next giant fish to skim my head. Here it comes from the east, straight for me. I shade my eyes and look up as it nears, its roar, already threatening. Can the pilot see me? If I wave my poppies will I distract him from the job in hand? The wheels seem in line with the top of my head, but now I am hypnotised as the outstretched wings and silver belly cover the sky. Defiant and deafening the sound blots out all memory and I have to duck my head, just in case. The thrill keeps me there for another half hour as jet after jet lands on the runway just behind me. Exhausted, I slide down the bank knowing that it is time to save the poppies from my hot hands.

Two Women I Imagine in 1920'S Montmartre

In the few hours I have in the middle of the day when the twins are having their siesta, the garden becomes my haven. I draw or read or write a letter home. After giving the children their tea I can sit here with Pascale on my lap and watch as Bea tries to catch her brothers. As soon as she disappears around the corner of the house, of course, I have to follow their screams and shouts.

One day Madame suggests that I might like to visit the city in the evening to see the display of lights, although I must promise to be home before eleven. I have an early supper and catch the six-thirty train. Changing at St. Michel and Chatelet I finally arrive at Place de la Concorde. As I begin my ceremonial walk up the Champs Elysee I imagine how it looked a hundred years ago.

Half-way to the Arc de Triomphe I get caught up with a crowd heading for a premiere night at the Lido and find myself within arms length of Elizabeth Taylor, Richard Burton, Maria Callas, and my heroine of the moment, Francoise Hardy. How could I know then that I would, in fifteen years time be having a heart to heart with Burton in New York. The red socks he wore were to remind him of Wales, he said.

PARIS A HUNDRED YEARS AGO

3

My mother writes to tell me that Aunt Eileen is in Paris visiting her sister, the one who is married to Col. Pallot. Their daughter, Dana is a Bluebell girl so actually works at the Lido! I must look them up. I know that this is my mother's way of getting some real information as to my state of health, as Aunty Eileen is known to tell all, with no frills.

I phone the number and am invited to tea on my first free day. Their apartment is in the posh 7th. *arrondissement.* At last I will see inside one of those elegant chandelier-lit buildings I have gazed at from the street.

At four o'clock a few days later I am walking into a classic Belle Epoque building and taking the ornate elevator to the third floor. When I press the bell at their front door I hear familiar voices as the aunts rush to greet me. I must now explain that these are not actual relations. In Wales we call anyone who is a close family friend, aunty *this* or uncle *that.* It is a nice tradition.

Once I am inside and seated comfortably the

aunts disappear into the kitchen to prepare tea and cakes. Col. Pallot is delightfully *English* and regales me with tales of his diplomatic life. I know that he was Forces Defence Advisor to the High Commissioner in Malaysia. His hobby is painting and on the walls I see very proficient examples of his work.

Dana, he explains, is still asleep. After two shows at the Lido and then supper at two in the morning she rarely gets to bed before dawn. However, at the rattle of tea cups she appears and walks sleepily to join us. After giving me a quick hug she collapses onto the sofa and begs a strong cup of tea.

An hour passes as I explain my new life in Ablon and my rather hazy long-term plans. I am much more interested in Dana. At eighteen her experiences are infinitely more exotic than mine. Of course, her looks are a tremendous advantage. She is five foot nine with long blonde hair and a figure to turn heads. After two cups of tea and a hefty slice of gateau she asks her dad to fix her a Dubonnet and soda. She has to start her evening's preparation and asks me to join her in her bedroom so that we can continue our chat.

Her room is as chaotic as mine at home although instead of my charity shop buys she has designer outfits aplenty. But, she does have to work for three hundred and sixty days a year!

At her dressing table she begins to 'put on her eyes', two pairs of lashes on her upper lid and one pair below. With foundation and powder and blusher she looks ten years older. At work she will add lipstick and gloss, gloss, gloss. She insists that I must come along to the Lido and meet the other girls. I am delighted.

Her cab arrives and we are whisked along and up the Champs Elysee to where I had stood a few weeks ago. Now I am a guest and we are ushered in like royalty.

The dressing room is a flurry of long-legged beauties in various stages of undress. I watch as Dana piles her hair on top of her head, adding false curls and twists until she tops it all with an enormous headdress of ostrich feathers and pearls. Her costume, although sparse, is heavy with diamantes and sequins. I am speechless.

Many of the girls are English – gorgeous visions

with broad Lancashire or Midlands accents. Others are Scandinavian or American. French girls are too petite, apparently.

Dana invites me to join them after the shows for the best cheesecake in Paris at the Café Lido, but that will be in six hours, and far too late for me.

On the way home in the train I am high on life's possibilities.

At eighteen Dana has such a glamorous life and such a salary! What do I want – money, fame or freedom? It doesn't take me a moment to decide that personal freedom is priceless. It is the one thing that I will defend fiercely for eternity.

The following week the Pallots ask if I am free to join them for a picnic in the forest of Fontainebleau. Madame agrees to change my free day as long as I take the children to the park for an hour before I leave. The park, with its bandstand, is my favourite local spot, but as it is another glorious day the children are loath to leave after only an hour's play.

When I finally herd them home the Col. and the aunts are waiting outside. Madame comes out to meet them and hands me a hamper of the usual good things to eat. While she chats to the family and introduces the children, I rush to my room to fetch my notebook and sketchbook.

Our first stop is Barbizon village, an enchanting fairytale of thatched cottages and ancient gardens. Deep in the forest I am sure that I see the Three Musketeers riding through the trees on their way to their next adventure. This is where Corot, Courbet, Millet, and Delacroix painted, the initiators of Impressionism.

The church is perfectly simple with whitewashed walls and white lilies.

The aunts have disappeared into the village shop, another magical image with its tiny windows, ancient shutters and worn steps. As I enter a bell tinkles and I step into a dimly-lit room which smells of sweets and lavender. On the satin smooth wooden counter sits the most magnificent cat I have ever seen, with eyes of turquoise and a ruffle of silver hair. Obviously so near the Chateau, this is the Queen of Cats.

Colonel Pallot has found us the perfect picnic spot, a clearing amongst the volcanic rocks.

Un Picnique dans le forêt du Fontainbleau

I am ordered to go off and sketch while the gingham cloth is laid out and the feast assembled.

It is difficult not be wax lyrical about life's events when everything turns out well, but food, atmosphere, wine and company on that day were of the best kind. Peggy's strawberry pavlova with a Cognac to follow topped the bill.

The Chateau of Fontainebleau does not disappoint in its majesty, and is less flamboyant than Versailles.

OUR TEA-ROOM

We take tea at Samois-sur-Seine, home of Mallarme and Django Rheinhardt, poetry and music and the sedate river flowing on to the sea. The Col. knows of an old farmhouse where they make *gaufres* – small thick pancakes dribbled with butter and served with a choice of *liqueurs*. It rounds up a day of pure pleasure.

It is strange that now I am on the same piece of land as the boyfriend, he seems more remote than ever. He is now settled somewhere at the back of my mind, and when he does wander to the front it is only to ask if I remember him. Letters arrive infrequently via home but I have experienced so many changes in my views and attitudes that I am not sure what to write in answer.

Of course, I tell him of my excursions, but what I want to impress, now that I am not under his intellectual domination, is that I am happier than I have ever been. Even with Madame's constant request to - please run to fetch fresh brioche, please iron the boys' school shirts, and please wash four faces and hands before presenting the children to the ladies who are taking tea in the salon, I am thoroughly content.

This would probably annoy him intensely. What am I doing to improve my education, he would demand to know?

So I enthuse about the architectural perfection of the gardens at Fontainebleau, the soaring arches of Notre Dame, the stained glass walls of Saint Chapelle, and my hours at the Picasso Museum. I am not turning into the little hausfrau he imagines. Every free moment I get I am sitting with pencil and pen drawing and writing, and dreaming of more foreign adventures.

I have my picnic lunch on the corner of rue
Daubenton outside this ironmonger's shop with its
fifteen foot shutters and gingham curtains blowing
in the breeze. In the afternoon I lose myself in
Paris' botanical gardens, Les Jardins des Plantes. It
is a perfect oasis of green.

Ablon Town Hall

Madame's Bedroom

4

Over breakfast one morning Madame asks if I would like to accept an invitation from her sister to visit the Drome, where she has a house in the mountains. I would be able to take the boys there for a month.

I have no idea where the Drome is, but just to see some mountain landscape will do my Welsh soul good. I say yes, and we begin to plan. She warns me that life there is fairly primitive so that it would be wise for me to buy any necessary items at the pharmacy. I understand and make the purchases I need.

We leave Paris on a sweltering summer day with Madame's last reminder that I use plenty of sunscreen on the boys as they will be out in the sunshine most of the day.

This is their first trip away from home, and I am pleased that their parents have so much trust in my guardianship. To cheer them up I open the lunch box early. Eating is a great distraction and soon the Rhone valley closes in and the landscape seems more inviting.

At Valence we are met by Claudia and Bonmama, the boys' grandmother. I am pleased that she will be staying with us as Claudia seems much sharper than her sister, and rather formidable.

We now take a local train to Pontaix way up in the foothills passing so many hamlets – tiny clusters of houses, a farm, and more goats than people. Our final stop is comparatively large with its station house, village store and deserted café.

We are greeted like visiting royalty by the stationmaster and his wife. There is only one taxi in the place and the driver ambles over to shake hands with us. He will take us the final five miles to our destination at St. Andeol.

All the way, as I get literally nearer to heaven, I am speechless with delight. The mountains get higher, the buzzards lower, and farm workers wave in response to the taxi's horn. The boys' tiredness gives way to excitement as they point out soaring cliffs they hope to be climbing!

When we finally reach Claudia's house way up above the village I remember Madame's warning regarding its remoteness. Only half the structure is complete. Claudia's husband is an architect and they are going to take years to finish this, their second home. We carry our suitcases up the steps to the large terrace where I notice that the date carved above the main door is 1768. Haydn, Mozart, and Bach were composing, while Schiller and Goethe were only in their twenties. Their names would have meant nothing to the villagers here in those days.

La Maison
Pontaix

This is my first mountain home where I will live like Heidi. This is the terrace where we will sit in the evenings to watch the sunset. On the bottom left is *le cavre* which keeps the fruit and vegetables and wine cool even in the noonday heat.

The stone is mellow and creamy like Cotswold stone but the effect is chunkier and rugged as a hillside home should be.

I wish the boyfriend could see this house, perfect in its location, blending with the creams and greens of the hillside. He could learn some lessons. I decide to send him a photograph with my next letter, just to get his professional opinion.

The kitchen, bathroom, and a room that Bonmama is using as her bedroom are all new, but our quarters are medieval.

I am to share the huge attic room with the boys so Claudia has fixed up a curtain to give me some privacy around my bed. The bed itself is a platform, and the mattress is stuffed with straw.

After a light supper the boys are soon begging to be allowed to go to bed. I see them settled and go down to have hot chocolate with Claudia. Her English is perfect, albeit with an American accent acquired from her Californian teacher. She has relaxed after a glass or two of wine and we talk of her worldwide travels with her husband. They have no children and I sense that she is quite happy with this as it allows her the freedom she enjoys.

At nine I excuse myself. It has been a long day. Bonmama calls goodnight from her room, and I climb to the attic happy as Heidi.

What wakes me at six-thirty the next morning is the faint tinkling of goat bells as the flock are led to the pasture above us. I look out through the tiny hole in the wall and see the mountains of the Vercors, pink in the early light. By seven the boys and I are bounding down the hillside to fetch the goat's milk.

My view from my hole-in-the-wall window

Monsieur Blanc is head of the village clan with daughters-in-law harvested from the surrounding villages.

With full churns of milk we make our way back to the house. As Monsieur has given us permission to pick up any windfalls of fruit on the path we manage to carry enough for dessert for the day. Claudia will steep these ripe apricots and nectarines in the local wine and a little sugar, and we will eat them with the goat's yogurt she will teach me how to make.

After breakfast Claudia shows me *le cavre* under the house. In the dark I smell ripening cheeses, fruits and strange mushrooms. She shows me how to strain the yogurt in a muslin cloth to make a creamy cheese. I wonder at the complexity of my life up to this moment. Surely, this is the way to live, simply and naturally?

I am free now to take the boys on a hike around the hills. They are hoping to see as many wild animals as possible, while I am determined to avoid all contact, especially with any snakes. As they race ahead I sing loudly to frighten away any lurking serpent intent on crossing my path. I have promised Claudia that we will return before noon so that we don't get scorched by the fierce sun. Buzzards swoop and glide around our heads but apart from birds and rabbits we see nothing dangerous. Running back down the hill is best as there is a slight breeze, and lunch is waiting.

Bonmama explains that Monsieur Blanc is Mayor of our tiny village. He has six sons who have all married girls from the neighbouring villages. There are fifteen grand- children and twenty two great grand-children. This family makes up the entire village.

Monsieur Blanc's eldest son is the sort of King of Pontaix, as he drives the only car. This serves as the taxi for everyone. If he is busy in the fields, we walk!

At two o'clock every afternoon all shutters are closed and the household enjoys a siesta. This is the chance I have to read the only English language book in the house. It happens to be the complete works of one, William Shakespeare, so it is all good stuff. Actually articulating English after only a few months away is difficult, but I also realise how much I have improved my French. I learn reams of speeches which I know will come in useful some day soon.

Claudia has made a point of saying, on several occasions, that it is hardly worth my while having a day off from my duties. What on earth would I do? But I have studied the local map and discover that an hour's train ride from Pontaix will bring me to the sizeable town of Die, the administrative centre of the department. I am determined to see it, and ask her if the following day is convenient for her to take complete charge of the boys. Reluctant as she appears to be, she cannot deny my request.

That evening, after dinner, I pack a lunchbox with goodies, and go to bed early. Too excited to sleep properly I know that I will have to be on the road at six to catch the first train to Die.

 Next morning I walk the five kilometres to the station in pristine air, picking up some apricot windfalls on the way. I sing my repertoire of Joan Baez songs and can't believe my good fortune in answering that advertisement months ago. Who would have thought that I would end up in this heaven?

At the tiny station I sketch a jumble of farmyard buildings. Part of the natural landscape, I pray that they will still be here in a thousand years in their splendidly distressed state.

The town of Die is bustling and for the first hour I feel quite out of place. Have I missed the chaos of humanity so much? I sip coffee in the main square and listen to the flow of conversation around me. The exchange of information appears to be still an art in France. It has none of the often dirge-like tones of British discussions.

If the French are complaining they do it positively and openly, and the subject is soon debated and over. Our grievances seem to have become part of the national psyche, like the British weather.

My second stop is at the local swimming pool where the water is warmed by the summer sun. I spend an hour lazing, and observe that my legs and arms are at last turning a healthy golden brown.

In the church on the square I light a candle for my family and spend some time in the cool silence contemplating where my life has brought me so far. Quite content with the situation I make my way outside to find a shadowed bench to have my lunch of homemade goat's cheese and Bonmama's sweet chutney in a crusty baguette.

For the following few hours I wander through the back streets of the town, taking a final coffee in a tiny corner café run by a family of seven who are all taking a late lunch in the main room. I sit out on the pavement enjoying the afternoon sunshine and musing on my future.

I sketch some exotic locations, and ponder. Do I take up that university place that has been offered?

I could take my degree in English and possibly become a journalist. Or should I study drama and return to my first love, dance?

Of one thing I am sure. I still want that place in France where friends and fellow artists can come and share some time, walking, drinking, talking, and working. We would be like Shelley and Byron and co., or perhaps more like Lawrence and his visions of his Ramadin. So maybe the Gulf of

Spezia would be better, or maybe Greece on some remote island? What a dazzling array of choices.

Heady with exercise and caffeine I make my way back to the station to catch my train home. I have promised to return in time for dinner, but I now have plenty of time for a leisurely walk from Pontaix. The sun is setting and the few farmers wave from the fields. They all know that I am *la jeune fille au pair d'Andeol.*

Over dinner I tell the family about my day's adventures, and hear that the boys have been quite naughty. They had turned the garden hose on Bonmama while she was taking a snooze on the terrace. There will be no treats tonight and it's early to bed! Madame seems rather fraught so I excuse myself as well, and spend an hour writing to my family who are due to take their own holiday in London. It worries me a little that I don't seem to be missing anyone at home as much as I had expected. Perhaps it is because my new life is so very different. How can I ever explain my daily joy of waking in this incredible air, eating such mouth-wateringly fresh food, and all within the security and care of this new family?

The following day Claudia is unpacking some boxes of books and finds a map of France which she says may interest me. I have loved maps since childhood, and I can read them for hours, pondering over new routes and contours, strange place-names and ancient sites.

I spend my siesta afternoon deciding where in France I should live, near mountains, or seaside, or both?

What excites me especially is the realisation of how close we are to the Mediterranean. Marseille seems a stone's throw away and I can see that I only have to get back to Valence to catch a direct train to one of the oldest ports in Europe. I have to see it. I have to get there!

Claudia, as expected, throws up her hands in horror. Marseille is probably the most evil city on earth, full of drug takers, easy women, and worst of all in her opinion, the U.S. Navy! Apparently, American ships are 'dry' with not a Martini in sight. That only means that when they hit dock the poor sailors are crazy for two things – alcohol and women!

My image of Marseille is now sizzling, but Claudia will only allow me the necessary two days off if she receives written consent from my parents.

That evening I am down in the village using the only telephone for miles. Of course, I know that my parents will still be on holiday, but my grandmother is a gem and always willing to back my adventures.

This time however, she hesitates. She has seen *The French Connection* several times! But she will be speaking to my parents tonight and she promises to do her best to persuade them to write giving consent.

I wait for ten days and hear nothing. Desperate measures are called for. Very early one morning I write a letter in my grandmother's hand giving Claudia reassurance that my sensible nature will not allow me to take any risks, and that a trip to Marseilles will only be to my educational advantage. Sealed in an old envelop where the date has been obliterated, I present it to Claudia. Her sigh is very heavy as she sees that she will have to care for her nephews for two whole days, *mon dieu!*

I try to hide my excitement from her by taking the boys on an extra long walk. This works well as they are then so tired that they plead to go to bed as soon as the last mouthful of pudding has disappeared from their supper plates.

Later I pour over my map again making a list of the towns I will travel through on my way to the beautiful Mediterranean.

A Letter from Home

5

On the appointed day, as dawn breaks, I leave the house. The train to Valence is at six thirty and I must catch it in order to make the first possible connection to Marseille. Excitement charges every muscle as I almost run the five miles to the station, a small knapsack of overnight provisions and a packed brunch on my back.

The journey itself is thrilling as the sun comes up over the mountains and I watch slices of life appear and pass as if in a dream.

As we skirt the Camargue the sky turns to charcoal and we enter the city assaulted by a violent thunderstorm.

Ever the optimist, I have brought no coat, so I spend my first hour in the station café picking at a baguette I had promised myself to eat with the Mediterranean at my feet.

I make a sketch of the palms bending to the wind, and add some colour notes.

The rain, bouncing on the hot pavements is somehow comforting, reminding me of home.

The city does not seem large and I am soon walking along the quayside of the old harbour in steaming sunshine. I can see the bars that Claudia has warned me to stay well away from. They look perfectly innocent at this time of day when the French are doing their serious eating, *a dejeuner* . Tonight, there would surely be no harm in taking a quick look, just for experiences sake?

I remember my unfinished lunch and head up the hill to the pinnacle where the Cathedral of Notre Dame de la Gare forms a crown.

Here the air is cooler and fresher and the view across the bay, stunning. Through the gaps between the medieval houses I get glimpses of the bustle of the new port with its enormous tankers carrying cargo to and from all parts of the world. Little do I suspect that within a few hours I will be on board the largest.

I sit in the Cathedral square. Finding my last biscuit I savour it, knowing that from now on I shall have to buy every morsel of food from my month's paltry savings. Suddenly my antennae are alerted. I am being watched by a sailor who is sitting nearby. He smiles. I look away. I look back and he smiles again. I look away again, but see, in time, that he is making his way towards me.

The stranger sits down beside me and stares at the view of the harbour. I stare at the same view and wish him away.

'*Bonjour, mademoiselle,*' he says in a voice as dark and smooth as chocolate.

'*Bonjour,*' I respond, to be polite.

'*Ah, tu est Anglaise,*' he says with some delight.

I am appalled that he can tell that I am not French from one tiny word. After all these months of daily practice!

'*Americaine?*' he tries.

I am determined not to waste my day in idle conversation.

'*Suedoise?*'

With my auburn hair and freckles this makes me smile, and just to stop the questions I announce that I am Welsh, *Galloise!*

This keeps him quiet for a few moments until he realises. '*Ah, tu habite a* Cardiff? That is good, as I speak good English.'

His accent is certainly excellent, and my curiosity, as usual, gets the better of me. Also, I want to put him at a distance. He had used the intimate '*tu*' form and I am determined to use the '*vous*'.

'*Et vous, vous habitez, ou?*'

'I am from Casablanca,' he says.

My mother's favourite film! I just have to turn and face him. His smile is generous, and the look in his eyes evokes the film's sultry heat, the romance, and the danger. I am hooked.

Malouf proves to be the perfect guide to the city and we spend the afternoon roaming streets I would never have found alone. By five o'clock we are near the entrance to the port and he proudly points out his true home, a dirty big tanker docked quite close to us.

He insists that I meet his mates, and knowing how much my father loves all manner of boats, I feel that I have to accept the offer. It is a thrill to know that in three days time this bit of metal will be touching into the port in Morocco.

After a brief tour we go down to the kitchen where Malouf promises that cook will feed me well. There are a strange looking bunch of men sitting around an enormous table, playing cards and drinking. The cook himself is minimally dressed and I begin to appreciate why as the heat here begins to melt my make-up. I am urged to sit and take a glass of beer. I decline the beer, but wait patiently as cook prepares something over the fierce stove. Malouf chats away to friends and is obviously enjoying my being there.

In a trice a plate appears before me loaded with the most inedible looking hunk of meat in a sea of fried eggs. There must be at least four! Starved as I am I only manage to eat two and a half eggs and a sliver of meat.

I wish I had a serviette to scoop the remainder into to avoid any embarrassment, but I just place my knife and fork in the correct positions and smile at everyone. Malouf explains why I am wandering around Marseilles on my own.

I recognise the word Cardiff and this does raise a smile as some seem to know where the Welsh port lies. One of the younger men pushes a bottle of rum towards me. A large measure is poured and everyone raises their glasses to 'Cardiff'.

The heat is beginning to encroach and I try to think of my cool mountain home. I smile at the man opposite me, but his toothless grin does not help. Neither does the sweet warm rum.

When cook asks if I am still hungry I nod, imagining some exotic Moroccan dessert. He returns, however, with another plate of fried eggs topped with a doorstep of grey bread.

With the heat and the smell and the runny eggs
I begin to feel rather faint, and beg Malouf to get
me out into some fresh air. The crew offer more
rum, but enough is *enough*.!

Gallant as he is we are soon walking in the old harbour towards one of those sleazy bars Claudia warned me about.

Malouf orders coffee and I feel safe again. There are already small groups of American sailors standing near the counter but they seem quite well-behaved. As I sip my coffee I realise that I have not booked a room for the night.

Malouf takes complete charge, guiding me up the hill where he says there are many inexpensive rooms to be had. We find a respectable looking hotel and he arranges the price of the room. It seems a bargain and I pay up happily. Now we are free to spend the evening watching the sun go down and the city lights come up.

The bars at the harbour-side are now full of marines downing alcohol as if the world is about to end. Malouf and I sit at a corner table and he insists that I join him in a proper beverage, a good Myer's rum. We are served with olives and salt biscuits and I relax at last.

Over the next few hours he tells me how good the crew are to him, treating him like a son after his father died suddenly three years ago. He would like to study more and maybe go to college in Paris.

I urge him to do so, telling him that I am hoping to return home soon to continue my education. Music comes from the juke-box and now one of the marines climbs onto a table and dances amongst the bottles and glasses. Everyone applauds, as he is actually very agile, though not Gene Kelly.

There are several glamorously dressed women at the bar and they seem to have chosen their partners for the night. Later, things get a little too boisterous as furniture is rearranged for dancing, and I long to take part. On the other hand, after a sixteen hour day, I am beginning to slump and tell Malouf that I have to leave.

Immediately, he is on his feet and guiding me through the crowd.

On the hill the night air makes me really drowsy and taking my arm Malouf almost carries me up the stairs to my room. I stop to open the door and it is then that he tries to kiss me, whispering endearments and leading us both into the room. I see that it is a double room that he has booked and I am suddenly wide awake.

'NO, no, no, no!' I shout, reverting easily to my native tongue as I push his lovely body out onto the landing.

Thankfully, he only plays the 'poor me, I will be all alone tonight act' for a few moments before bowing low, and asking if we might meet for breakfast.

He has been such a good companion that I have to say yes, and I thank him for a very memorable day. As I close the door behind me I have to smile at his intentions, honourable or not.

Now, the utter weariness returns and I almost crawl towards the bed, throw back the covers, and collapse into semi-slumber. Half-heartedly, I brush what I believe to be a fly from my arm, and throw back the flimsy sheet, for it is incredibly warm. I think of getting up to open the window but am distracted by the same fly, now on my leg. Then there's another on my head and I sit up, annoyed that I can't be allowed to sleep.

Struggling to the light switch I turn it on, go back to the bed, and see the horrible sight of several insects marching across the pillow. I reach for the under-sheet and pull it back to reveal a swarm of fat, black, crawling lice. I scream and drop the cover back on the bed. I wait in the eerie silence, but no one comes to my rescue. No wonder the room was so cheap. There was obviously no extra charge for the lice.

My knees buckle with exhaustion as I realise that I will have to spend the whole night on a tiny bentwood chair with my feet propped up on the sink. Maybe I should have listened to Claudia after all. I longed for my straw mattress under the leaky roof. Dawn cannot come too soon!

At the sight of the first flush of a new day I splash cold water on my arms and legs in an attempt to revive myself, and escape. I walk away from the harbour side, east towards the Corniche. I had made notes from the municipal map of the location of *Cite Radieuse*, Corbusier's masterpiece, something I should see now that I am so close. This is not just to impress the boyfriend, but for my own education, and to justify my thoughts on modern architecture.

As daylight arrives I am walking along the promenade with the dark blue Med. on my right. The sea and cool air restore my enthusiasm, and energy. Within fifteen minutes I see Le Parc Borley on my left. I cross the promenade and enter through ornate gates.

The trees are magnificent and I sit for a few minutes to sketch, although hunger is gnawing at my insides. When I spy the awning of a café down the street I immediately taste the *café au lait* and *pain au chocolat.*

Trees in Parc Borley, early morning.

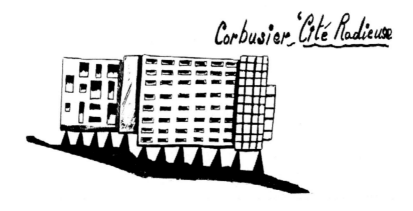

Corbusier 'Cité Radieuse

A BLOCK OF CONCRETE

What utter disappointment! Have I walked miles to see this? Not quite as repugnant as bed-lice, but still, pretty ghastly if one had to live here. A block of grey concrete marked with uniform windows and doors painted in vivid primary colours.

I do a crude sketch for the boyfriend. I will make it clear that I strongly opposed to putting people in chicken coops, and if this is his idea of architecture our relationship won't last a month!

On my way back into the centre of the city I see this example of harmonious architecture. It could easily be adapted for many families.

Without realising it, I make my way straight for the railway station. I can't wait to get back to my life in the mountains. I have an hour to spend before a direct train will take me back to Die. A superb omelette and glass of wine in the station buffet restores my equilibrium. After all I am saving on a night's accommodation, with or without bugs!

I draft a letter to said boyfriend where I extole the virtues of the *Belle Epoque* and urge him to remain the romantic I first met. When I re-read it I realise how confident I have become.

At home my charges are in bed and sound asleep so I creep up to join them and rejoice in the comfort of my straw mattress. How a little travelling re-asserts your priorities!

This is what I will have the next time I visit the South of France, a room with a view. The muslin curtains will billow into my room bringing rays of sunshine across my bed.

I'll watch the sunrise and sunset as the Med. turns from aquamarine to ultramarine and the palm tree darkens to a silhouette.

6

After only three more weeks of idyllic mountain life we are on our way back to Paris. The Blanc family organise a party in our honour and I shall never forget the warmth and generosity of this isolated community.

After a few days in Ablon we make our way to the family house at Anizy, north of Paris. Grandpapa lives here year round, but every holiday rooms are opened for the arrival of the whole clan.

As we drive north I am amazed at the lush greenery in the fields and woodlands. It refreshes my eyes.

Madame explains that the house was requisitioned by German soldiers during the war. They built barracks in the vast garden and used the barns to store ammunition. There are still marks on the dining table where they chopped their meat. While the countryside looked flat and uninteresting these facts stirred my imagination, and I looked forward to hearing more.

It is a dream house, nestled in woodland, protected by high walls and elaborate gates. The terrace at the front has chairs and tables enough for twenty, and is surrounded by a magnificent rose garden.

There is a flurry of greetings as the family meet brothers, sisters-in-law, cousins, aunts, and uncles. We are shown up to our rooms, or in my case, *room.*

It is a vast attic space which I am to share with the four children. The boys are delighted with their far, dark corner where a heavy velvet curtain has been attached to an oak beam to give them the 'out of sight, out of mind' atmosphere they need.

In the middle of the room, under a sky-light, are the twins' cots. I can imagine them waking to the first streak of dawn so I plan, as soon as possible, to arrange the cots away from early morning light.

My corner has been divided off, and I am pleased to see a vase of fresh country flowers at my bed-side.

My first introduction to the house is through Oriette, our Catalan cook who has been with the family for aeons. She is absolute monarch of the west side of the house with its enormous kitchen, pantries, laundry, *le petit bureau*, a sort of office for the administration of all household requirements, and *le fils*, a small room alongside, where I am to feed the children their breakfast and lunch. Dinner, I gather, is a formal affair, and while the boys will attend, the girls will be fed and abed before aperitifs are served.

Oriette guides me through the range of pots and pans that I should use for the children and helps me prepare a simple supper for the girls. Not having fed them for many weeks they think it quite a hoot that we three are sitting at a scrub-top table in this yellow room with green gingham curtains. They are delighted by their high-chairs, family heirlooms painted in blue and pink. I wonder how many bowls of pureed vegetables and custard puddings have been served here. How many irate parents or maids have wielded spoons into open mouths or played games, waiting for determinedly shut mouths to open?

While Pascale is easy to coerce, Beatrice is adamant that she will not eat a morsel. Seeing this, of course, Pascale, who adores her sister, absolutely refuses as well. I am as tired as they are after the long day's journey so I quickly serve up dessert without any feelings of guilt. This sweet creamy mix goes down a treat and we are soon climbing the stairs to bed.

Having tucked them in I am wishing to crawl into my own bed, but I must change into the only dress I have, and see that the boys are presentable for dinner. My prime motivation is a raging hunger which over-rides my anxiety at meeting the whole clan at one sitting.

When we reach the salon it is filled with chatter and laughter. Madame calls us over to a sofa where I sit with the boys who have become extraordinarily shy. I am served with a glass of Pineau, a sherry type drink from Charente, Madame explains. The boys have fruit juice.

A tall, tanned boy comes over to introduce himself as Marcel. His sister, Francoise, and he are here for a month. His English is impeccable as he has studied for two years in Oxford. Do I cycle?

Yes? In that case he will have a bicycle ready for me by the weekend and they will show me the countryside about. It rolls gently so there are no heavy hills to negotiate, thankfully, because most of the bikes in the barn have no brakes and certainly, no gears!

A heavy gong sounds from the hall and as Bonpapa's bulky silhouette crosses the glass doors between the salon and the study, we all get to our feet and follow him into the dining room. There seems to be an unspoken acceptance of the hierarchy in the family as everyone makes their way to stand behind their chairs. As the eldest son, Monsieur sits next to Bonpapa and as soon as they are seated we sit. I have followed Madame and the children to the far end of the table where she sits at the head. Eduard and Antoine are to be each side of her and I am next to Antoine. Opposite me is *Tante* Lara who gives me a wink and a generous smile. Do I look ill at ease?

There is a hush as Oriette serves *le potage* helped by a young girl from the village. Antoine, overcome by the silence, starts to giggle but is immediately tapped on the hand by his mother.

The wine is poured and tasted. The boys are given a small portion which is topped up with water. They sip this as if it is vintage brandy. Bonpapa gives them a warm smile and nod as he watches them.

It is only after the dishes have been cleared that the atmosphere seems to soften. The talk gathers pace and I am struck by the vivacity and dominance of the women, such confidence and sophistication.

After the main course has been cleared Madame asks me to take the boys upstairs to bed. They are immediately obedient, kissing their mother before walking the length of the room to kiss their grandfather and father. There is a general chorus of, *'Bonne nuit, petits.'* as I escort them from the room.

When I return to the dining room two vast plates of cheeses are being circulated. There is a great interest in the choices being made and when my turn comes I am perplexed by the six or seven on offer. I take a portion of dependable Brie, some walnuts, and a small bunch of grapes. I really must be more adventurous. This is my chance to savour the unknown.

Lara is talking to her cousin about the joys of the English countryside. She has lived in London for ten years, teaching French in the *Lycee* in Kensington. I think that she will be a good friend. She has travelled the world and is helping the family in writing the history of the house. She has visited most of the Welsh castles and wants to know more about my country.

Madame thanks me again for looking after the boys so well in the Drome. I have obviously been a good influence. She will be happy to write me a reference if my future husband needs one. I laugh and shake my head at the possibility of marriage, yet looking around the table at this picture of a happy family I realise that it has always been one of my dreams to have my own two boys and two girls. If I could replicate this atmosphere I would be more than content.

When Bonpapa gets to his feet everyone does likewise and we follow him through to the salon where coffee will be served. There is a discussion of the arrangements for the next day. The two barns still need to be cleared and Lara reminds everyone how many of the family treasures are still buried there. Soon after the outbreak of World War Two as the Germans had advanced, paintings and antiques had been boxed and hidden.

I ask Lara about the knife marks in the dining table and she takes me back into the room where the oilcloth under the tablecloth has been washed down, dried and rolled up. Deep hatchet marks are prominent in the wood. I touch them and shiver. It seems so recent now, all that horror.

The next morning the twins are awake at six, but they are quite content to talk to one another in whispers for almost an hour. I listen, trying to make out the sense, but I drift in and out of sleep, happy to know that they seem to understand each other perfectly.

When I finally wake with a start it is seven thirty and I am suddenly energised by the idea of exploring this amazing house and its ten acres of garden. I call the boys but find that they have gone, dressed but unwashed, probably in search of Oriette and sustenance.

The twins are both angels this morning and as I carry them down to *le fils* I smell fresh coffee wafting from the kitchen. Oriette is there and serves me a slice of baguette and home-made cherry jam. She tells me that the boys have been fed and are out with Lara in the barns.

The twins eat their cereal with relish and I am free to dip my bread into my coffee and taste the unique combination of flavours.

I think of all the people who have lived here over three centuries. It feels that, discounting the war years, the house has always been loved. The twins are not two years old yet. I just hope that they will be bringing their children and grandchildren to stay each holiday in Anizy.

While Madame takes the twins out onto the terrace, where Bonpapa is having his coffee, I decide to pick up some cooking tips from Orriette.

Orietta dans sa cuisine.

The Perfect Country Kitchen.

An hour passes easily as I talk to Oriette and beg to copy some of her recipes. She is delighted to lend me her kitchen 'bible' from which I can choose my favourites.

She offers to give me a tour of the house, and takes off her pinafore before ushering me out to the main corridor.

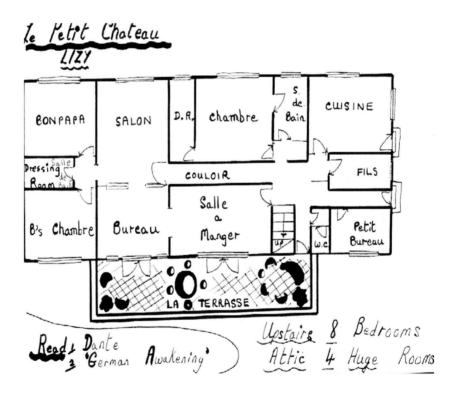

A Rough Plan of the Chateau

My quick sketch shows the basic layout, with Bonpapa's apartment in the east wing. The windows are massive and there seems to be an array of shutter designs. The floors are parquet and gleam like glass, and everywhere are cupboards, shelves of books, and window seats wide enough to curl up in on rainy days. I am in love with this house.

Upstairs are eight bedrooms, dressing-rooms, bathrooms of marble, and in the attic, four huge rooms. Some of the cousins are sleeping in the barracks in the wooded area of the garden. It is only in the summer and at Christmas that every space is occupied.

I am drawn back to the kitchen with its enticing aromas, dappled sunshine, hanging bunches of herbs, onions, garlic, glinting copper pans, and, of course, Oriette, who is always, always busy.

If Madame takes the twins to play in the mornings and the boys are away with their cousins, I help Oriette with her preparations. Truth be known, I was never very interested in cooking when I lived at home. Always deep in a book I never seemed to hear my mother's calls to come and see how to make a sponge, or pie.

Now that I am here in foreign climes I want to learn, and Oriette is a patient teacher. I watch the potatoes par-boil before turning them out into a bowl and putting them near an open window where they will cool in time to be slathered in home-made mayonnaise for lunch, or sautéed in hot olive oil. I am asked to fetch ingredients from the massive pantry which does not have a convenience packet of anything! There are sacks of flour, jars of ground nuts, a variety of sugars and teas, row upon row of conserved vegetables and fruits all with their handwritten labels in immaculate script. On a marble slab there are four cooked hams and two enormous baked salmon dressed with swirls of herbs and twists of lemon. What seems like two dozen eggs are piled in a bowl ready for tonight's dessert, *Ile Flottante,* which I am eager to learn how to make.

Oriette invites me to join her in feeding the chickens. I follow her out to the kitchen garden and beyond, where chickens and rabbits roam freely within their large compound. I throw the corn and chickens come scrabbling to eat. Without a word of warning Oriette grabs one poor bird by the neck, swings it between her knees where it is trapped for a second before its death by strangulation. She lets the body drop to the ground and although mindful of their fate the other chickens still cluck around Oriette's feet. She is obviously the mother goddess who comes each day to feed them, talk to them, and cosset them. I shoo my lot away, but not before three more have been slaughtered. This is enough of a rural lesson for me today. I am off to prepare lunch for the twins, and will definitely not choose the pureed chicken.

The countryside around Anizy, as Marcel promised, is perfect for cycling. As Monsieur has arrived from Paris to spend the weekend with his family I am free to take off with the cousins. There will be five of us in all so Oriette packs us a picnic lunch. I carry my sketchbook and some pencils just in case there's time to draw.

My latest sketches are of imagined scenes on the beautiful Mediterranean. Francoise is keen to see the sketches I have done since my arrival. She has always wanted to study art.

She wants to hear all about the boyfriend, but frowns when I stress his extreme confidence. Haven't I met any French boys? Don't I find them attractive? I explain how sorely tempted I have been, and how impossible it would be to have any kind of relationship while living 'en famille'.

We cycle for two hours before stopping by a woodland stream, a perfect picnic spot. I am beginning to relax in the family's company, overcoming my hesitation as I pronounce the new

French words I have learnt. In front of the children I am happy to make a fool of myself, but these cousins are my age and their English is flawless.

The soft red wine helps my shyness and we are soon chatting away like old friends on every subject under the heavens, and all in correct English. It is Marcel who asks me how long I am planning to stay. Obviously, I do not want to make a career out of childcare.

'No, of course not,' I remonstrate. 'I have so many plans. I want to do a degree in Literature or Journalism. I want to travel. I want to live in Paris for a year, and then Italy. I want to visit America, coast to coast. I want…I want…I want….'

Everyone laughs with me as I run out of wishes. Francoise brings the boyfriend into the equation, but he suddenly seems totally irrelevant. Where exactly would he fit in amongst all my wonderful plans?

That night as I fail to fall asleep I realise that I will soon be nineteen and really must decide on a course of action. This comfortable existence with no challenges or risks will not nourish me for long.

Tomorrow I'll talk to Tante Lara. Her life has been constant change and I envy her. She took charge and made definite decisions.

Of course, the following day when I go in search of Lara Francoise tells me that she has gone to Rheims to visit friends, but she will be home on the weekend. Now, I can't wait for the weekend!

The following few days are wet so I take the four children to play in the barracks tucked away in the woods in the far corner of the grounds. This was built by the German soldiers who took over the village and made it headquarters for some time. It is an eery place for me, but the children love it. The rain batters the roof and I close my eyes to sense the history of the place.

As soon as the sun reappears we are out of there and indulging in the harvest of raspberries, gooseberries and strawberries in the kitchen garden. As their bathtimeI I have to drag the twins away, luring them with promises of their favourite treats for supper.

This is not one of my usual subjects but she came out of my imagination so I could not resist.

Over the weekend I borrow some books from the study and sketch the exotic architecture of Monte Carlo. With my watercolour set I make colour notes so that, one day, I can complete the paintings.

This more opulent end of the south of France will have to wait for another trip. I realise that I will have to save quite a sum before I am able to sit here on the terrace of the Hotel de Paris sipping a martini or climb those steps to the casino doors.

I work on a painting of Monet's garden which I might present to Madame. She has said how much she loves, Giverny.

Immediately I see it as a parting gift. Guilt then creeps in as I realise that I have not even been here a year. How can I leave so soon?

This is Le Petit Trianon where Marie Antoinette played shepherdess to her own flock of sheep.

I have only weeks to decide whether or not to take up the university place which I have been offered. Of course, my father was right all along. Art College was wrong for me, and University could be the best option, especially as I am so unsure of my career choice. I hear Lara singing as she works in one of the barns, and I pluck up my courage, knowing what I want her to say.

Her response to my question is immediate.

'Of course you must go to university! Do you want to be changing nappies all your life?'

'So what should I do now?'

'Tell Madame today so that she has time to replace you, then accept your place at college and start packing.'

How simple it sounded coming from somebody else. As I thought of the best time to make my announcement my friend, Karen, came to mind. She had been so envious when I had told her of this French adventure of mine. Karen's only ambition has always been to be a super mum, so this would be the perfect place to practise.

Madame and Monsieur are sitting on the terrace enjoying an evening drink when I venture to tell them of my decision. I stumble through with many apologies and end with such a glowing description of Karen's superlative nurturing skills that Madame asks me to ring her immediately.

Within the hour my life is turned about and my path ahead full of opportunities, timetables, and excitement. Karen gives an immediate, 'Yes!' Although her French is quite poor she will put in a month's hard study.

I phone my parents and ask them to make the necessary calls. My mother's voice falters and I realise how worried she has been about my future plans.

I write to my pen-friend, Colette. We have been exchanging letters for ten years and now that she is so close I must see her. She lives with her family in Ay, a village near Epernay, home of the best Champagne. Within a few days she phones to say that she will be delighted to meet me at Rheims if I can get a train there from Laon. The cathedral should not be missed! I can stay as long as I wish.

For the next few weeks I really enter into family life. I help Lara scrub the copper pans that she has found buried in the barns. On the occasional rainy day I sit with all the cousins as we darn sheets made of heavy Egyptian cotton and talk of life's oddities. I take down as many of Oriette's recipes as possible, and take the boys cycling around the country lanes. All these activities make me more dependent on everyone, and I lie awake at night realising how much I will miss them all, especially the children.

On the other hand I cannot wait to be free, to see Paris again, and to be with my own family in Wales. The boyfriend will be back at college in a few weeks and I am not at all sure of my feelings in that direction.

The final goodbyes take a whole day. Oriette packs me my favourites for a train picnic and Lara says that she will drive me to the station at Laon. I have exchanged addresses with the cousins, and the boys give me a brief hug before bounding off to the barns to see what else has been unearthed. Knowing that there is a separation in the air the twins begin to cry so violently that Madame has to take them indoors.

At Laon Lara waits while I buy my ticket, then, with a warm embrace she is gone, sounding the horn of the car as she leaves the station yard.

Colette and her fiends are at Rheims to meet me,and allow me plenty of time to wander through the Cathedral. It is a gothic dream.

We have tea before we drive to Ay. Again my French is faltering as I try to convey my pleasure in meeting her at last. We have gateau and coffee and plan the few days I have here.

There is a fete in the village on the following day so there will be plenty of entertainment and fun. I can't imagine attending a similar event at home, but am happy to fall into any of her plans.

Ay is a small and friendly village and I am given a large glass of champagne at every meeting. Colette's parents speak no English, but are so hospitable it makes no difference.

I wear my one and only dress to that evening's events where everyone, young and old, dance to perfection. By midnight I am worn out by the wild French waltzes and too much bubbly. We have sausages on warm bread before making our way home. I warn Colette that I may sleep until noon on the following day.

Sunday lunch is sacrosanct and the small dining room bursts with family members discussing the success of this summer's fete. We spend the afternoon walking the fields on the gently sloping hills surrounded my miles of luscious vines.

That evening we meet up with a crowd of her friends who chat away quite happily in English for my benefit.

With Colette in college the next day and her parents at work in the vineyards I decide to leave for Paris.

Monsieur Renault drives me to Epernay station where I can catch a direct train to Paris. More goodbyes and good wishes all round, and I am off again speeding west towards the city where it all began.

7

I find a bed in a youth hostel on the left bank, and am free to explore with no trains to catch or children to worry about.

The aroma of fresh baked bread leads me to Paul's, what is now, all these years later, my favourite café. It has butter-cream walls, a pale grey dado, worn carpets, and over-sized chandeliers. Each table is made of a different wood, some seating two, some seating twelve. The staff are discrete and the service faultless. Not that I ever mind waiting for a glass of frothy milk topped with a miniature hazelnut meringue.

On my first visit I request the milk because it is the cheapest drink on the menu. The tall waiter bows low to ask if I would prefer honey or vanilla to flavour the milk. I know then that France is a different world.

A Russian couple come to the next table and soon we are deep into a discussion of twentieth century writers. I tell them about Shakespeare and Co., and how, every Monday evening, there are readings by contemporary writers from all parts of the world. They will certainly visit the bookshop as soon as possible. I leave them to enjoy their strawberry tartlets.

I wander through the narrow streets, buy peaches from the market stall, and find myself in the perfect Paris square tucked behind the church of St. Germaine. I sketch Place du Furstenburg quickly but will not finish this as a painting for years.

I eventually completed this from a magazine. The article celebrated the opening of Manuel Canovas' new Paris store. It would be another fifteen years before I would meet him in New York.

The September air is balmy and the golden leaves send dappled sunshine over everything. I pass Le Procope, the oldest restaurant in Paris, founded in 1686. I have read that it was here that Voltaire set up a record for drinking twenty-four *café-chocolats* in one day. Assuming the place closed for a few hours, that must have made two or three an hour!

I make my way to one of my favourite corners of Paris, the chair in the upper window of Shakespeare and Co., overlooking the Seine and Notre Dame. As usual, the bookshop itself is crowded.

Someone is playing the piano in the back room, some haunting pieces reminiscent of Michael Nyman's work. The pianist is David and comes from a village three miles from mine back home in Wales. He has been in Paris for months, and should have returned home by now.

MY CHAIR WITH A VIEW

Upstairs, in the library, my chair is free, and there are fresh flowers on the velvet covered table.I find Henry Miller's, 'The Happiest Man Alive', James Joyce's letters, and 'The Confessions of an Art Lover', the biography of Peggy Guggenheim.

With this inspiration, my notebook, the flowers, and the bells of Notre Dame sounding the hour I am at my happiest.

Two hours later I read that Peggy's collection of Braques, Delaunays and Klees have been rejected by the Louvre as not being worthy of storage space. It is imperative that she leave Paris for a safer home. Hitler has just invaded Norway, and France is next on his list. Italy has declared war on France, and Peggy, being Jewish, must fly. She packs her car with paintings and drives south and out of the city.

I notice that each chapter of the book begins with, 'The end of my life with...' and not, 'The beginning of my life with...'

It is her recklessness in love and life that intrigues me, and I am fascinated by the fact that she had a brief affair in the thirties with Humphrey Jennings, ten years before he chose our Welsh village as a location for his film, 'The Silent Village'. It was an unusual time for the people of Ystradgynlais, being cast as 'extras'.

Jennings used my grandfather's darkroom to produce the stills for the film which told of the destruction by the Germans of the people and village of Lidice in Czechoslovakia.

©PMH

UPSTAIRS AT SHAKESPEARE AND CO.

I open Joyce's Paris letters at 1920. He is complaining of the cost of running a hundred lamps and gas stoves to keep out the winter cold. It is an expensive address, number five, Boulevard Raspail, and already he has spent twenty thousand hours on Ulysses. The problems are just beginning with printers, and publishers. Humour abounds however. He mentions that in Switzerland he was recommended to consult Dr. Jung, the Swiss Tweedledum, as opposed to the Viennese Tweedledee, Dr. Freud.

Ready for a drink I make my way to the nearest café, away from the tourist throng on the Quai. It is near the Sorbonne and filled with students and aged professors. I sit in a corner and over a café au lait I enjoy the scene.

The French don't seem to mind being stared at,
and this is the perfect model.

Picasso
1904

I think of Picasso arriving here when Paris was at her artistic height.

How intriguing the city must have been then, what adventures to be had, what discoveries to be made. Picasso is immersed in his Blue Period and Symbolism. Next year there will be an uproar at the

Salon d'Automne, all caused by the Fauves and their work. Led by Matisse they were the wild animals of the art world. Madame Matisse, with a green stripe down the middle of her face begins a revolution. *Vive la revolution!*

The following day I walk through the Tuileries Gardens, across Place de la Concorde and up the Champs Elysee. I have to buy my mother a bottle of Guerlain's Chant d'Aromes perfume and I *must* buy it in the Guerlain shop. I have put on the same, one and only dress, so that I feel more the part as I enter the exquisite boutique and am served most graciously by a woman swathed in sophistication. She wraps my purchase, a small Eau de Toilette, carefully in layers of perfumed lilac tissue and ties it with gold threads as if it has cost a thousand pounds. I can't wait to present it to my mother.

LA PLAZA ATHENEE

Here is where we may stay one day, one of the most sumptuous hotels in the whole of Paris.

I make a list of the hotels I would choose in the city and find that at the top of the list comes the Hotel des Grands Ecoles off Cardinal Lemoine. It is next door to where Joyce lived and near Henry Miller's rooms. It is tucked away up a cobbled lane and sits surrounded by trees and rose- gardens.

The hotel is also near the first road into Paris

from the south, the narrow and bustling rue Moufftard where the food markets are a treat to behold. On my first day here there was dancing outside the church with everyone from toddler to grandpa up and waltzing . Only in France!

Fermette Marbeuof, an Art Nouveau wonder.

Here, I dare to ask the manager if I might sketch. He is all charm and I promise to send him a print of the finished painting.

As I walk along the boulevards I often see myself entering a restaurant and seeing my man of the moment with another woman. Or is it me at the table not knowing that my escort is already spoken for!

BOULEVARD ST. MICHEL

This is the scene I will always visualise as I think of Paris, the boulevard cafes of the Left bank. With the aroma of fresh coffee, the chatter and bustle, the waiters in their long aprons, the flirtations and quarrels it encapsulates this city.

This is someone I should like to know better, Monsieur Marcel Proust. I have only dipped into *A Le Recherche du Temps Perdu* and found it a rich canvas full of atmosphere and symbolism.

As soon as I get to college I shall tackle it again with more seriousness, I promise myself.

This is where we friends will meet each evening.

MONSIEUR AND MADAME CHAGALL

A couple I would love to have met. I am reminded of the Russians I met at Paul's, intelligent, sensitive, and generous. I make a note to visit Nice as soon as I am able to view Chagall's work at the chapel in Vence.

His paintings are narratives, symbolic of so many of mans' journeys, out of Eden, out of his country.

AT THE RITZ

I walk back via the Ritz and nip in to experience its seductive warmth. This temptress is worth remembering for a future painting.

On my last evening I treat myself once again to a Café de Flore coffee and sit on the terrace watching, just watching, as the autumn sun tips the trees with vermilion light. I sip my coffee slowly and keep the napkin as a souvenir.

It is impossible to imagine myself back in Wales with my family. Will they see how I have changed? I am a good deal slimmer, certainly a little tanned, but it is my mind that I has altered most.

Soon I will have to be searching for a flat to share in Cardiff, hopefully in the same lovely street where I spent my year in Art School.

Then it will be a reunion with the boyfriend. That is something I am going to stage-manage perfectly. I have written the script a hundred times over the past few months, and am determined to show him this new and confident self. After all, I will soon be meeting a mass of new students from all corners of the world, and I need to be free to live my life exactly as I wish.

This is Simone de Beauvoir writing in the upstairs salon of the Café de Flore. What an inspiring place to think with good coffee at the ready. Peace and inspiration go a long way to producing a masterpiece.

This is elegance, a glamour which Paris inspires. How can artists capture light on denim and cotton tee-shirts? Where is the sheen of satin, the gleam of silk, the ruffle of pleats? I was born in the wrong era.

I wander back to my small room on this last night of my first French adventure watching the lights come on in those high windows.

I see that the ego will loom too large in modern architecture. There will be no soul and very little heart put into design. I will have to keep an eye on the boyfriend's plans!

Early next morning as the bus transports me to the airport I concentrate on every doorway, every cornice and cobbled street. I wave goodbye to the Tour Eiffel realising that I have not yet been within its shadow. There is so much more to see, to hear, to taste and understand that I promise to return soon.

AU REVOIR PARIS.

CAROLE MORGAN HOPKIN

Everywhere she goes she carries a notebook and sketchbook to record as much of her surroundings as possible. Born, brought up and educated in Wales she has danced with Sinatra, dined with Buzz Aldrin, supped with the Beatles, and travelled many miles on foot over rough terrain.

In this series of travel books the pictures tell as much as the text about the world through the eyes of an artist.

OTHER PUBLICATIONS

FULL CIRCLE   Gomer Press 1995

THE SENSUALIST   Gofannion Press 2008

THE SENSUALIST

'You won't have read many books like this before. It's racy, funny, and atmospheric.' Steve Dube. *Western Mail.*

DRAWINGS and PAINTINGS available from **www.morganhopkin.co.uk**